"Two stems up!"

—*Pumpkin Times Magazine*

"The most awesome book of 2021...
and maybe even of ALL TIME!"

—Brandy's dad

"This book is so good—I'm officially
buying one copy for each eye! Arrggg!"

—Captain "One-Eyed" Louie, Pirate of the Seven Seas

"A delightful read...it has everything: words,
commas, exclamation points, pictures,
occasional poor use of grammar,
and did I detect a hint of nutmeg?"

—Random guy on the internet

THE PECULIAR BOOK OF PUMPKIN POETRY

Pumpkin Carvings and Poetry
by Brandy Davis

Illustrated by Brittain C. Scott

LUMINARE PRESS
WWW.LUMINAREPRESS.COM

Printed in the United States of America

Illustrations by Brittain C. Scott

Luminare Press
442 Charnelton St.
Eugene, OR 97401
www.luminarepress.com

LCCN: 2021918059
ISBN: 978-1-64388-770-8

Dedicated to
dreamers,
children,
and the forever children at heart.
Magic exists within you.

Snorty Gourdy

Snorty Gourdy loves to laugh
He laughs at everything
He laughs until a snort comes out
And more laughs it swiftly brings

He just can't stop those snorts and laughs
So he's now in quite the rut
And then it happens—he laughs so hard
That he cracks himself right up

Leaky Lou

Leaky Lou had a leak or two
So when he drank juice
It would leak right through

There were some things
Leaky Lou could not do
Like drink his juice and barbecue

It really was such a shame
Because his juice would spill out
And douse the flame

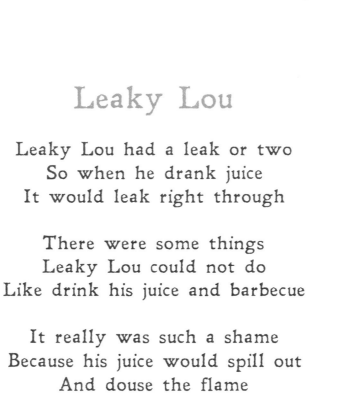

How Pierre Became a Millionaire

Artist Pierre sat in his chair,
Wishing to become a millionaire...

So he painted one million pictures
Some bigger and some smaller
He wrapped them up nicely
And sold them all
Each for one dollar

Gilly's Garden

That Green Thumb Gilly
Some say he's a bit silly
For growing those pumpkins so

And although it may seem strange,
Or even downright deranged
There is something most don't know...

While others may scoff
Or point fingers and mock,
His garden, he still tends

The reason he toils
In the dark and dank soil...
All he wants is a true pumpkin friend...

Itchy Ritchie

Ritchie is itchy and covered with spots
And boy, those spots itch an awful lot!
There are spots on his back and on his hands
All this itching Ritchie can't stand!
They're all over his face and on his stem
Ritchie scratches again and again

He scratches high, he scratches low
He scratches fast, he scratches slow
Will this itching ever stop?
Probably not...Ritchie's got the Pumpkin Pox

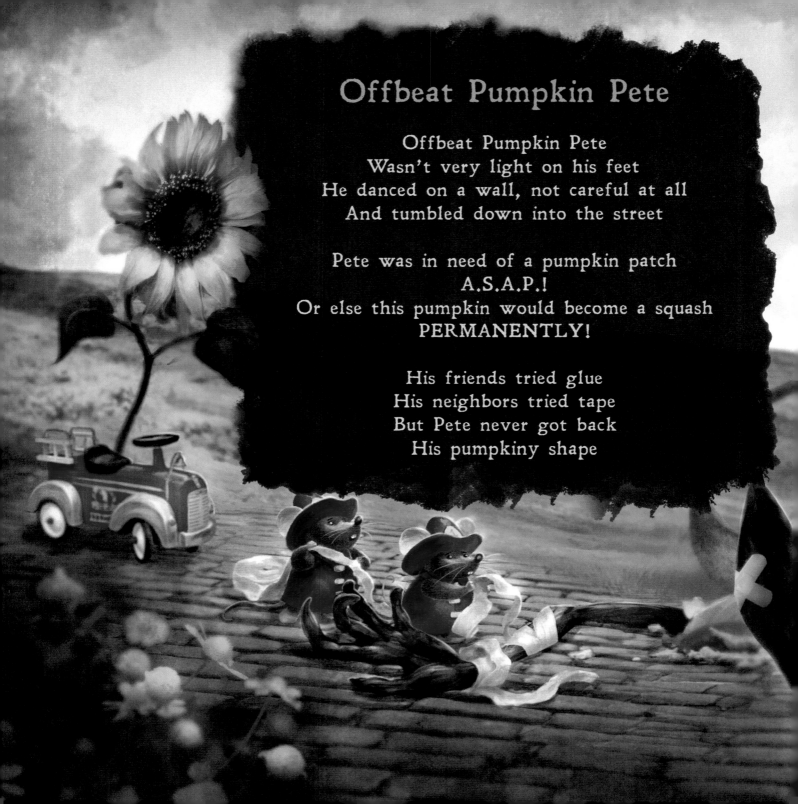

Offbeat Pumpkin Pete

Offbeat Pumpkin Pete
Wasn't very light on his feet
He danced on a wall, not careful at all
And tumbled down into the street

Pete was in need of a pumpkin patch
A.S.A.P.!
Or else this pumpkin would become a squash
PERMANENTLY!

His friends tried glue
His neighbors tried tape
But Pete never got back
His pumpkiny shape

Sour Sammy

Sammy Shane Sullivan O'Shea
Loved to eat lemons every day
Sometimes lemonade or lemon meringue pie
Even lemon spaghetti or lemon french fries

He loved the tart, he loved the sour
Sometimes whole lemons he'd devour
His lips would pucker and his eyes would wince
His face would scrunch from the bitterness

Until he noticed that one day
His lemony face just stayed that way
Now, whether he eats lemons or not
A sour face is what Sammy's got

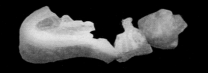

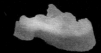

Sleeping Stan

Sleeping Stan sleeps all he can
For a very clever reason
You'll find him sleeping throughout the year
And through every kind of season

If you try to wake him up
He will surely kick and scream
'Cause he simply loves to stay asleep
And dream of Halloween

Pumpkin Pie

My name is Timothy Nye
And I despise pumpkin pie!
For obvious reasons,
No need to say why!

Besides, why would you eat it?
There are better pies to be had!
Like chocolate or peach,
Even key lime isn't so bad...

Strawberry-rhubarb,
Or apple pie à la mode!
Even chicken pot pie,
Sure! Have one of those!

But please, not pumpkin pie
For your next sweet treat...
Because it might be Timothy Nye,
In the next one you'll eat...

Exit Poem

Did you know that pumpkins are
A squash, a gourd, and a fruit?
Not to brag, but we are quite unique
And the things we say are too

Now that you've read our book,
I'll teach you a phrase or two
Because you're part of our secret pumpkin club,
The Peculiar Pumpkin Crew

So listen up!

When the best day of the year rolls around,
And we wake up from our dreams,
We jump out of our patch and yell with joy,
"Oh my gourd-ness! It's Halloween!"

As the day comes to a close,
And the sun is no longer bright,
Before we pumpkins sleep and doze,
We say a very dear, "Gourd-night"

And as this peculiar pumpkin book,
Sadly runs out of time,
We'd love if you came back to visit again,
So we say, "Gourd-bye...Till next vine!"

THE MAKING OF THIS PECULIAR BOOK

The *Peculiar Book of Pumpkin Poetry* is peculiar indeed! Unlike any other book you may have seen...(wait, that wasn't supposed to rhyme...).

Every pumpkin character you see within is actually a photo of a real-life pumpkin carving by professional 3D pumpkin carver Brandy Davis. Each pumpkin took her eight to ten hours to carefully carve and set up with props and special lighting. On most pages (though not all), even the pumpkin's vine arms and legs are real, posable props made by Villafane Studios. Several other props in the scenes, such as the pumpkin canvas painting, beret, and paint palette in the poem "How Pierre Became a Millionaire," are also real-life props handmade by Brandy. Many hours of detailed artwork went into these scenes, but it didn't stop there.

To really immerse the pumpkin characters in each of their stories, the unedited photos were then skillfully superimposed into digitally rendered scenes designed by professional illustrator Brittain C. Scott. The result was this peculiar book of whimsical artistry and humorous poetry, creating an extraordinary, one-of-a-kind world of Halloween, pumpkins, and magic.

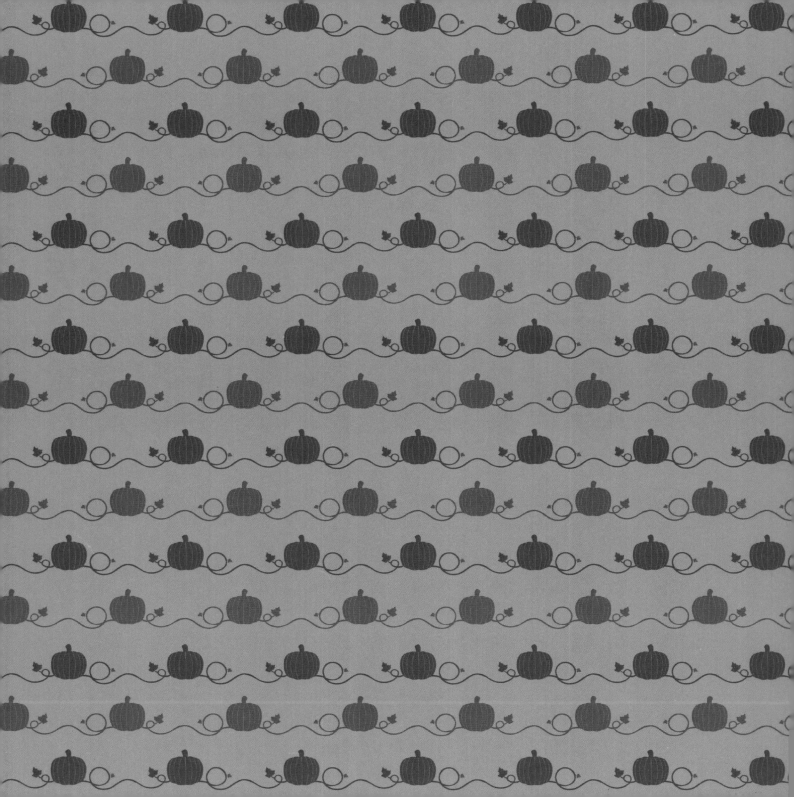

ABOUT THE AUTHOR

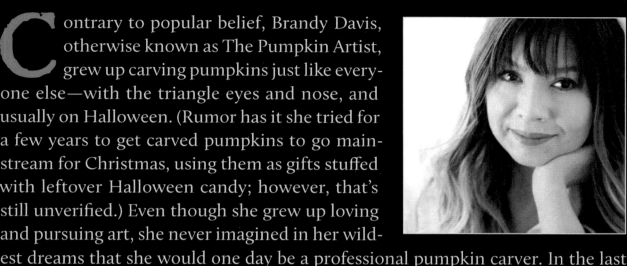

Contrary to popular belief, Brandy Davis, otherwise known as The Pumpkin Artist, grew up carving pumpkins just like everyone else—with the triangle eyes and nose, and usually on Halloween. (Rumor has it she tried for a few years to get carved pumpkins to go mainstream for Christmas, using them as gifts stuffed with leftover Halloween candy; however, that's still unverified.) Even though she grew up loving and pursuing art, she never imagined in her wildest dreams that she would one day be a professional pumpkin carver. In the last decade, she has been a 2018 Guinness World Record Holder for the Largest Jack-O'-Lantern ever carved (2,077 pounds!), competed on Food Network's *Halloween Wars* and *Outrageous Pumpkins*, and is now co-creating this peculiar book with an amazing artist who is about to become the president (see bio on next page).

She still regrets not finding out about the awesome art of 3D pumpkin carving sooner—like that first time she tried a maple-bacon doughnut and thought, "Where have you been all my life?" Today, Brandy is making up for lost time and continues to carve her award-winning 3D pumpkins for various prestigious venues and companies all over the continental US, gathering her widespread acclaim for her talent. And even though she wrote the poems in this book, she offers a disclaimer: "I'm not a poet—I'm just a pumpkin carver with a sense of humor. My only hope is to bring a smile to the face of anyone who is in need of a surge of fun, inspiration, and magic in their lives—for children and the children-at-heart."

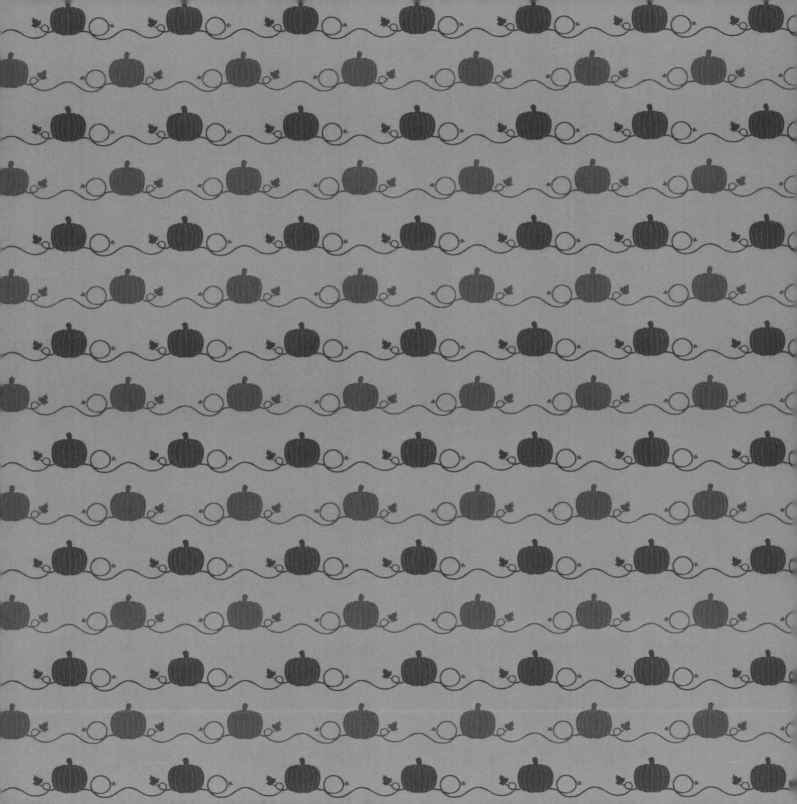

ABOUT THE ILLUSTRATOR

Brittain C. Scott's mom told him he could be anything he wanted to be when he grew up. After years of deciding whether he wanted to be an astronaut, the president, or a secret agent, he decided to be an artist because the other jobs were just too difficult. Drawing came easy to him, so naturally it was his calling. However, after a number of years working as an artist, he is reconsidering the president job again...maybe the secret agent too. During his time as an artist, he has worked in video games, film, and publishing—many of the projects bizarre. Although this is his last artistic endeavor before he becomes the president, he hopes you cherish this book he has worked on with Brandy Davis.

TILL NEXT VINE!...

Made in the USA
Las Vegas, NV
19 October 2021